Kid
Youtuber

By Marcus Emerson

ALSO BY MARCUS EMERSON

Diary of a 6th Grade Ninja
Secret Agent 6th Grader
The Super Life of Ben Braver

This one's for Elijah...

Emerson Publishing House

Book design by Marcus Emerson
Art created digitally in Clip Studio Pro.

EPISODE 1:
I'M KIND OF A BIG DEAL

I mean, we grew up playing videogames so that pretty much makes us experts at everything. If I can get first place in Mario Kart, then I'm PRETTY SURE I'll be fine driving to school.

I've actually got TONS of brilliant ideas like that. I don't want to brag, but I'm SUPER smart. I even got an "OFFICIAL GENIUS" score on a test that was on the back of a cereal box. I framed the award that came inside it, too.

Anyways, my name is Davy Spencer, and you're watching my first YouTube video!

MOST first episodes are boring, but not mine. This one is AWESOME so hit that Fan button and share this with your friends because today I just got...

Wait for it...

MY NEW CAR!!

It's the new Cobra Spitfire that doesn't even come out until NEXT YEAR, but I got mine early because I'm kind of a big deal. And now that I have a brand-new convertible, I'll be the coolest kid in town.

Babes love guys with nice cars, ask anybody. All I have to do is drive with one arm out the window and one hand on the wheel.

But after messing around with it, I'm sad to say that, besides being a convertible, there's nothing else special about the car.

Maybe I'm being picky here, but there's no grappling hook launchers. No jet turbine engine. No armor plating. And no rear oil slick dispensers.

And if I had more time, I would've taken it out for a spin around the block, but I had to stop filming pretty quickly right after that.

EPISODE 2:
I LIVE IN A MOTEL

Ø1 VIEWS   Ø FANS

Someone at this motel left the top down in their convertible.

I saw an opportunity and I took it.

What can I say?

I'm an entrepreneur.

And yes, I said MOTEL because that's where I've been living for this WHOLE summer. I've had to share a room with my mom, dad, four-year-old sister, and her blind dog Bo-bo, who, by the way, is a 14-year-old toy poodle, which is like, a hundred in dog years.

Krissy really loves that dog. She even wears little dog ears so he feels like he's got a little doggy friend even though he can't see them because he can't see.

4

My family's been on vacation before, so it's not the first time we've shared a room, but THIS is NOT a vacation. This is torture. This is some sort of alien experiment to see which one of us goes crazy first.

I'm pretty sure it's gonna be my mom.

My dad got a new job at the beginning of the summer. Because of that, we sold most of our stuff, packed the rest in a tiny trailer, and moved across the country. My dad tried to make the trip fun by stopping at tourist spots, but they were only places that HE cared about seeing.

Now we're living at a place called the El Rancho Motel until we find a house, which is taking WAY longer than my parents said it would.

My sister and I are SUPPOSED to share the second bed, except she peed in her sleep every single night for the first week we were here, so I've been on the cold, dirty floor ever since.

It's not the cleanest spot in the world, but nasty carpet is better than a pee-soaked bed any day.

The motel has a pool, too, so that's pretty cool.

The water is a darker shade of green than I'd like. Plus, it smells fishy. And you can't see the bottom. And the top has so much grime that it looks like you can walk on it. But my dad says it's still cleaner than lake water.

And there's free coffee and donuts in the front office every morning. I don't drink coffee because it's nasty, but I've been known to take a donut or two. Oh, but just so you know, taking MORE than that will get you in trouble. The motel employees hate it when you do that even though their sign CLEARLY says it's allowed.

I've made a couple friends my age here, too.

The first one is Chuck Metropolis. His name sounds like he's a cop from the future. His parents are the owners of the El Rancho, but Chuck thinks that means HE owns the place, too, which can be pretty annoying sometimes.

Chuck also wants to be a ninja when he grows up, like that's a real thing you can go to school for. His goal in life is to practice 10,000 ninja kicks or something, I don't know. I thought he was trying to break a world record, but Chuck said it's how a real-life ninja named Bruce Lee used to train.

Chuck wears his ninja costume under his real clothes so he's always ready to become a ninja just in case we're ever surprise-attacked by OTHER ninjas, which might be a problem here? I'm still new in town, so maybe I haven't been around long enough to see it happen yet.

On really quiet days, you can hear Chuck kicking trees and counting behind the motel. It's a little weird.

And the second friend I made was Annie Yun. She lives right next door to the motel with her parents and four younger sisters. And I thought I had it bad with ONE sister.

Annie's the best artist I know, but that's not hard since I don't know a lot people yet. She spends all day drawing monsters and goblins and other weird things in her sketchbooks, but then she tears out the pages and crumples them up afterward. She told me that it's because she's a "TORTURED ARTIST" – her words – but I think she's just trying to sound cool.

She's says she's acutely aware of the subconscious corporate influence that "girly" styles have on her work and tries hard to subvert the expectation her parents have set for her to make drawings of unicorns or rainbows. She chooses, instead, to fight the system by drawing unicorns FARTING rainbows.

The worst part about living in a motel is that I don't have any of my stuff, and my stuff is very important to me.

It's my STUFF, y'know what I mean?

My toys, my videogames, and yes, I've even started missing my books. They're ALL sitting in a storage unit somewhere just collecting dust until we find a home, which doesn't look like it's gonna be anytime soon.

I'm not sure how much longer our family can take a one-bedroom living space.

Anyways, without my stuff, this has been the summer that won't end. I'm actually LOOKING FORWARD to school starting because then at least I'll have something to do.

I know that sounds crazy, like, I hate summer vacation, but trust me, doing nothing is better than having nothing to do.

The only thing that's kept me from going insane has been watching YouTube streamers playing videogames.

It's not the same thing as actually playing, but at least it's something.

That sounds about as smart as showing a picture of food to a starving person, but I'm surprised at how much those streams itched my videogame scratch. My sister even does it, but instead of watching gamers, she spends HOURS watching other kids play with their toys.

So we'll watch videos on Mom's phone until the battery dies, which she's never happy about, even though she's always telling us to give more than we get.

PHONE'S DEAD. DAD ALSO TEXTED A BUNCH OF STUFF ABOUT AN HOUR AGO.

HE WAS SUPPOSED TO TEXT ME WHEN HE NEEDED A RIDE HOME FROM WORK!

After my mom took her phone away, I asked if I could just get my own. That way, she wouldn't have to worry about hers dying all the time, which is a win-win if you ask me.

But I didn't come right out and say, "Hey, can you buy me a phone?" Doing that would've gotten me a big ol' "NO," which is what I try to avoid most of the time.

There's a delicate process to follow when you want your parents to spend money on something that's TRULY important to you.

I find that it's best to give an honest presentation with reasonable bullet points. My dad sees through it, but my mom eats it up every time.

WHY I NEED A PHONE

i do not want to die of boredom

DEATH BY BOREDOM IS A SERIOUS ISSUE PLAGUING TODAY'S YOUTH, RIGHT BEHIND DEATH BY EMBARRASS-MENT.

everybody else has one!

IF I'M THE LAST KID TO GET A PHONE, THEN MY RISK OF DEATH BY EMBARRASSMENT SHOOTS THROUGH THE ROOF! YOU DON'T WANT ME TO DIE, DO YOU?

Don't you want me to have a better childhood than the one you had?

YOU'D BE SURPRISED AT HOW MUCH THIS ONE WORKS.

But even after those solid points, my parents STILL said no because "we live in a motel, and money is tight right now." Then they said if I was REALLY nice, maybe I could get it for Christmas, but that's WAY too long to wait.

The next day, my dad came home with a beat-up digital camera he got from a guy at his office for free.

I'm not sure if my dad understands that a camera is NOT the same thing as a cell phone, but that doesn't surprise me since most adults don't really get technology.

I didn't want to make him feel bad, so I acted like it was cool.

The camera was older than me, but it still works and even has a memory card. My dad was excited about it because he thought maybe I could be a photographer or something.

But I'm not really a "photography" kind of kid. I just can't see myself taking artsy pictures of sunsets or anything.

Besides, I don't want to be the guy BEHIND the camera – I want to be the guy in FRONT of it. And after taking a closer look at the one my dad got for me, I found a tiny button that made that possible.

The button that records videos.

Every brilliant person remembers the exact second in their life when they had their greatest idea of all time. Mine happened in the tub.

Well... ABOVE the tub.

In a hundred years, people will line up to visit that bathtub because it's the EXACT spot is where I, Davy Spencer, figured out what I wanted to be when I grew up.

EPISODE 3:
THE SECRET TO FAMOUSNESS

Ø1 VIEWS   Ø FANS

Becoming famous is almost impossible for any normal person, but lucky for you, I'm NOT normal.

I'm the total opposite of normal.

Anti-normal?

Counter-normal?

Nevermind, you get it.

Most famous people get that way for being awesome at one thing, right? Actors are great at acting, singers are great at singing, and rock stars are great at rocking.

But you see, the problem with ME is that I'm pretty awesome at EVERYTHING, so it's kinda hard to choose what I want to become famous for.

And since I don't want to waste a bunch of time trying to figure it out, I'm just gonna skip all that and become famous overnight on the Internet. All it takes is ONE video to go viral and the whole WORLD will know who I am.

How cool would it be if I started the first day of school as the new kid who everybody ALREADY knows?

So THAT'S what my vlog is all about.

It's my real-life rise to fame that you can watch. I'll use my camera to record the videos and my mom's laptop to edit them. After that, she'll upload them to YouTube for me, and then it's just a matter of time before I'm the most watched kid on the planet.

And your entertainment will ALWAYS come first. Nobody wants to watch boring videos, which is why I'm gonna add some spice to mine.

Nothing TOO crazy, just enough to keep my Fans interested.

Chuck and Annie already said they'd help. Chuck will do some filming; Annie will mostly work with the editing. She's also gonna add interviews to my videos so there's footage of people saying how awesome I am and other cool stuff like that. The best vlogs have those kinds of honest moments in them.

My face is gonna be everywhere. TV. Newspapers. Internet. Soon, the whole world will know who Davy Spencer is. I'll be the greatest kid who ever lived, and everybody will want to meet me. I'll never have to stay in another crummy motel for as long as I live.

All I need is for ONE video to go viral to kick things off.

Ø1 VIEWS   Ø FANS

EPISODE 4:
JUST A LITTLE OFF THE TOP

He **DID NOT** love it, but I think it's because he's too old to appreciate a good joke. He really needs to learn to lighten up.

EPISODE 5:
FIRST DAY OF COOL

Ø1 VIEWS   Ø FANS

I caught Krissy filming a tea party with her blind dog before school this morning. They were both wearing matching cowboy outfits - hats and vests and everything!

I put a stop to that right away because that camera is MY claim to fame, and I can't risk her breaking it with her clumsy little kid fingers.

Or even worse, what if Bo-bo barfed all over it or something? He's getting up there in age. It could happen. Then it would stink like dog barf.

GROSS.

THAT is exactly why I NEED my own bedroom again. And sharing stuff is unfair because she always wants MY stuff!

It's never the other way around!

MOM SAID THE CAMERA WAS FOR **BOTH** OF US! WHAT IF I WANT TO MAKE A VIRUS VIDEO, TOO?

Anyways, today was the first day of school. I got up at 6:30, fixed my hair, brushed my teeth, and put on my best suit because my dad always says, "First impressions are important."

And dressing better than everybody else guarantees that I'll impress THEM before they impress ME.

Everybody will be like, "Hey, who's that cool kid in the suit?" and then Chuck or Annie will say, "Oh, that's Davy. He's that kid on YouTube." And by the end of the day, I'll be the most IMPRESSIVE kid in the school.

THOSE CLOTHES ARE GONNA GET YOU BEAT UP.

NOBODY WOULD PUNCH A KID IN A SUIT!

REALLY? BECAUSE I KIND OF FEEL THAT URGE RIGHT NOW.

Starting over as the new kid from out of town is the perfect opportunity for me to become whoever I want because nobody knows me yet.

I'm like a blank slate. An empty canvas. A fresh pair of socks.

The kid I was at my old school doesn't matter because THIS is my fresh start.

My new school is called Wood Intermediate, and it isn't far from the motel, so Chuck, Annie, and I walked. My suit made things a little warm - small price to pay to look so good - but once we got there, I had to find some shade because the doors didn't open for another ten minutes, and I was DRIPPING with sweat.

But even though I was hot, I still played it cool for everyone that walked past me.

I've only uploaded a couple videos to YouTube so I knew I wouldn't be swimming in a sea of Fans on my first day of school. But with Chuck and Annie's help, I was very optimistic about my SECOND day of school.

We'd spent the night before making important business materials in the motel office. I'd Xeroxed my face a bunch of times so I could hand out autographed headshots that had my YouTube information on it.

As soon as the doors opened, everybody went inside. Annie left to find her locker while Chuck and I handed out my headshots to anybody that would take one.

WHO IS THIS?

THAT'S DAVY. HE'S GOT HIS OWN VLOG.

OH, THAT KID WITH THE VLOG? I THOUGHT HIS NAME WAS... FRED? FERD?

FERGUS!

UH, NO, MY NAME IS DAVY.

That was SUCH a good sign because even though those kids got my name wrong, they all KINDA knew who I was. And at this point in my career, I'll take it.

I mean, it was the first day of school, and people were already KINDA talking about me.

Getting famous was gonna be easier than I thought.

Wood Intermediate is a pretty big place. It's two-stories tall and looks as big as an airport inside. There are tons of kids, too, and tons of kids means tons of new Fans.

I also have to say that there were some things I'd never seen before in a school, like vending machines for students, a huge mural that went all the way down the hall, and a kid duct taped to the wall.

I don't think he was part of the decor.

Chuck told me that getting duct taped is what 8th graders do to 6th graders and is definitely something we want to avoid. It's a way of getting branded as a dork, which is the exact opposite end of where I want to be on the popularity scale. I guess duct taping has been going on so long at Wood that it's become a tradition.

I found my locker right outside the cafeteria, which was like hitting the jackpot because it was a nice, open spot where the WHOLE SCHOOL could see me. And the cute girl in the locker next to mine was just an added bonus.

You hear that? She liked my suit.

Chuck gave Emma a headshot while I told her all about my YouTube channel and how it was gonna be the coolest thing on the Internet. And she totally would've been into it if it weren't for the giant SLUG who showed up from outta nowhere and RUINED my moment.

His name is Dutch McKenzie. He's a 10th grader stuck in 8th grade. I know that sounds impossible, but there he was, a foot taller than me with sideburns and the beginning of a beard growing on his chin.

I don't know how he was still in middle school. You'd have to ask Annie.

DUTCH STARTED KINDERGARTEN A YEAR LATER THAN EVERYBODY ELSE. AND THEN HE GOT HELD BACK IN 4TH GRADE, WHICH PUTS HIM TWO YEARS BEHIND WHERE HE SHOULD BE.

Dutch just kind of stood there quietly, like he was waiting for me to FEEL his presence. And what was the first thing he said to me?

GIVE ME YOUR LOCKER OR I'LL POUND YOU INTO DIRT.

Straight to the point — a real go-getter. He's the kind of kid who knows what he wants and just TAKES it from whoever has it. There was no messing around with him.

Good thing I had a ninja in my squad. At least, that's what I thought. When I looked back at Chuck, he was gone. I have to give him some credit though, he vanished like a professional ninja. I thought he would've JUMPED at the chance to practice a ninja kick or two, but he totally bailed on me.

So without Chuck, I only had two options — get beat up in a nice, open spot where the WHOLE SCHOOL could see me, or give up the best locker ever and my possible future wife. The choice wasn't hard because you don't test an 8th grader who probably drives himself to school.

The worst part about it was that Dutch didn't swap his locker with mine. He wanted BOTH of them, so I had to carry all my books in my backpack. By fourth period, my bag ripped open from all the textbooks, which didn't surprise me because those things weigh about 15-pounds EACH.

I've had that backpack since third grade. We've been through everything together. School, vacations, camping trips... I was gonna give that backpack to my son when I grew up. And now that'll never happen because of Dutch McKenzie.

After that, I went to the front office to see if they had any extra backpacks in the Lost and Found, but all they had was a carry-on bag with wheels – the kind that drags behind you as you walk.

I begged the secretary to check again, but that was all they had so there I was... the new kid dressed in a suit and pulling luggage behind me to each class. You know what I looked like?

The rest of my day wasn't much better. I already have homework for every single class, which is wrong on so many levels.

The first day of school should be a day of rest and relaxation. Kids need to get used to summer being over and EASE back into the daily grind of boring classes.

Most of us have been sitting on our butts for three months, and a sudden change in a routine like that is actually hazardous to our health.

This is something I strongly believe, and I know I'm not the only one. Everyone in science almost had a heart attack when Mr. Mitchell told us to start planning our project for the science fair because it was only ONE MONTH AWAY. That's barely enough time for our bodies to get used to waking up early again!

And then there's Physical Education, which by the way, is just a fancier name for gym because it looks more official on a report card.

Everything about middle school phys ed is just strange.

Apparently, students are supposed to bring extra clothes to wear for class because they expect us to work up a sweat right in the middle of our day.

I guess I missed that memo.

And did you know there's a group shower in the locker room that we're actually expected to use? I had no idea it was there until some kid walked out of it, naked and wet.

I could also be wrong, but I'm pretty sure the showers are for AFTER class when you're all sweaty.

Phys Ed is taught by a mighty woman named Miss Gymalski. She's the most muscular person I've ever seen in my life. She's from Austria and used to be an Olympic weight lifter, and she doesn't let anyone forget it.

She's got pictures of her glory days all over the gymnasium. And she points at them during warm-ups to motivate us to work harder.

Anyways, since I didn't have gym clothes, I had to sit on a bench and take an F for the day. Can you believe that? I was at Wood Intermediate for LESS than a day, and I already scored an F. That's gotta be some kind of record.

And, yeah, it was a bummer, but it was nothing compared to what happened next...

38

EPISODE 6:
FERGUS THE HORRIBLE

That's Fergus Widdershim...

His name sounds like somebody spilled a bowl of alphabet soup.

I'm only showing you a clip of his video so you can see how much he loves himself.

Wouldn't want to give him the views, like he even needs them, look at his Fan count! 212!

He's like a rockstar!

Anyways, there he was, sitting next to me in phys ed. At first, I thought he was cool. We had a lot in common. We play the same videogames, watch the same TV shows, we both love cheeseburgers, and we actually got along great... until I brought up my YouTube channel.

And you know what he said to that?

Get this, he said...

And then I realized that everyone who passed us in the gym was saying hi to HIM, but not to ME, which was the opposite of what should've happened. I learned pretty quick that he was practically the most popular kid in school, and it was because of his videos.

EVERYBODY knows him. EVERYBODY loves him. EVERBODY'S friends with him. AND he's FAMOUS. And it's all thanks to his vlog.

Does any of that sound familiar? It should BECAUSE IT'S EXACTLY WHAT I'M TRYING TO DO.

Fergus stole MY IDEA before I even HAD it! I'm not saying he's from the future and traveled back in time to use my own ideas before I could, but is there any way to prove that's not EXACTLY what he did? Every possibility should be considered. That's just good science, so... he MIGHT be an idea thief from the future.

You know what I think? I think he's paying for the views. You can do that, you know. It's not illegal, but I'D never stoop so low. The NERVE of that kid, right?

Fergus' channel has everything, too – food reviews, a day in the life segments, crazy wheelchair stunts, professional edits, amazing graphics. I mean, c'mon! Leave a little something for the rest of us! I'm not the only one who thinks that either. I'm pretty sure Chuck and Annie feel the same way.

Fergus HAS to have his own production crew. There's no way one kid can do all that on his own, so right there, he's cheating.

And then after he found out about my channel, he wouldn't shut up about it. He kept telling me how to get more people to watch my stuff. He ran his mouth the whole class, trying to give ME advice about what kind of videos I should make, like I need ANY help at all.

Please, Fergus, I was a BORN to do this.

He even followed me around after gym, introducing me to everybody and telling them to check out my channel, but it was all an act.

It HAD to be because nobody's THAT nice in real life.

UUUGH! You see?

If Fergus' plan is to kill me with kindness, it isn't gonna work because I'm smarter than that. I know who he really is and what he's really doing. He's a wolf in sheep's clothing – a bad guy PRETENDING to be a good guy.

He even subscribed to my channel. Obviously, so he can rip off MORE of my ideas.

But you know what? In a way, I'm glad I met him. His videos made me realize that I need to take mine up a notch. Or a BUNCH of notches. I'm gonna give it everything I've got by throwing ALL my noodles at the wall to see what sticks.

EPISODE 7:
PAST BEDTIME WITH DAVY SPENCER

Ø2 VIEWS   1 FANS

It's almost midnight, and our first guest comes from Sheboygan, Wisconsin! He's been roaming the country for twelve years and is starting his career as a stand-up comedian on my channel TONIGHT! Ladies and gentlemen, please welcome TRAINCAR JIMMY!

EPISODE 8:

SCHOOL LUNCH INGREDIENTS THAT WILL SHOCK YOU

I had this idea that it would be really cool if I reviewed hot lunches in the school cafeteria. Not every day, but at least once a week. I believe incoming middle schoolers should know what they're getting themselves into.

School lunch is something all students have to deal with, no matter who you are. If you go to school, you gotta eat in the middle of the day, right?

It's something kids around the whole WORLD can relate to. And relatable videos are the key to making it big on YouTube.

So, for lunch today, it looked like tacos were on the menu.

I say it "LOOKED LIKE" because you never know exactly what you're getting with cafeteria food. Just because something LOOKS like food doesn't mean it IS food.

What exactly is the school trying to cram down our throats? Is it some criminal evidence that the lunch lady needs to dispose of in the stomachs of middle schoolers? Shredded up counterfeit money that she was told to "get rid of" by some higher-ups?

Whatever it was, it was NOT tacos. I mean, look at this...

A DECONSTRUCTED TACO

That's about as far as I got with my food review because Chuck showed up and told me that kids were starting to stare.

What Chuck doesn't understand is that stares are good! Stares meant that kids were starting to take notice of what's going on around them – mainly that they're witnessing the birth of an influencer.

Stares meant I was getting attention, and attention leads to becoming famous.

Which, y'know, is the whole point of my channel.

I was getting so much attention that someone even gave me a compliment AND their apple.

And right there, in that moment, is when a little light bulb flipped on in my brain, and I had an outrageously great idea. An idea so simple it was stupid.

The GOOD stupid – not the BAD stupid.

It was gonna be the most ultimate food fight in history, and I was gonna film the whole thing on my camera. All I needed to do was scream "FOOD FIGHT!" while throwing my taco at someone's face. And then everybody in the cafeteria would join because that's what happens in movies all the time.

Chuck and I had to come up with the plan by ourselves because Annie was too afraid of getting in trouble. She didn't want it to go on her permanent record, even though I'm pretty sure there's no such thing as a permanent record.

Chuck and I took our food and moved to the table where all the cool kids sat. They kept their eyes on us like we were up to no good, probably because we were totally up to no good. But it didn't bother me that they were suspicious because the only thing that mattered was the food fight.

And that's when I did it.

I grabbed my taco, stood up, and screamed at the top of my lungs.

I threw my taco across the table at a hundred miles an hour, setting it on a crash course for Chuck's nose. Everything was on track for the plan to work flawlessly – I had everyone's attention, the cafeteria was full of students, my camera was rolling.

But then Chuck messed up the whole thing by NINJA-DODGING my taco. He leaned back as the taco went right over his nose and slapped the back of some other kid's head at the next table.

Chuck kept saying he was sorry, but what was done was done!

Instead of the lunchroom breaking out in an epic food fight that WOULD HAVE TOTALLY gone viral, everybody just stared at me and the kid with greasy taco meat sliding down the back of his neck.

Of course, it couldn't have been just some random kid I hit either. It had to be the WORST PERSON POSSIBLE because my luck is THAT bad.

I've never run so fast in my life.

But I didn't get far. Just as I got to the doors, Miss Gymalski caught the back of my pants with her massively muscular hand. Then she pulled me up, giving me an accidental wedgie in front of EVERYBODY, including Emma Walsh, who was at her locker with her friends. It was one of the most embarrassing moments of my life.

And I got it all on camera.

I got in-school detention and Dutch got a free shirt from the school because I ruined the one he was wearing. I didn't get the viral video I wanted, but at least I still had all my teeth.

EPISODE 9:
THREE SECRETS ABOUT DETENTION PRINCIPAL HAWKINS DOESN'T WANT YOU TO KNOW

EARLIER TODAY, I TRAVELED DEEP INTO THE DEPTHS WOOD INTERMEDIATE WITH A HIDDEN CAMERA TO BRING YOU FOOTAGE OF **IN-SCHOOL DETENTION!** VIEWERS WITH WEAK STOMACHS SHOULD TURN AWAY NOW BECAUSE THE FOLLOWING IS FOR **MATURE** AUDIENCES ONLY.

MR. HAWKINS

Ø2 VIEWS   2 FANS

#3: Old Man Garrick

Detention is run by a retired teacher named Mr. Garrick, or as other students call him, OLD MAN GARRICK, who might be a real-life vampire.

He's pale, crazy skinny, and looks like he combs his hair with an angry cat. All that, and his teeth are EXTREMELY white.

Tell me, WHY would his teeth be so white if he WASN'T a vampire?

The first thing Mr. Garrick had me do was hold up a mini chalkboard that had my name and violation written on it. Then he took a picture of me and stuck it on the wall next to a bunch of other photos of kids doing the same thing. You know what those kinds of pictures are called? MUGSHOTS.

#2: <u>Forced</u> Manual Labor

After pictures, Mr. Garrick ordered everyone to grab a garbage bag because we were going outside to do the community service we owed our school.

He even made us wear orange aprons, probably so we'd stick out if we tried to run away.

We were out there for at least an hour, picking up every piece of trash we could find. We were allowed to take breaks with ice-cold water whenever we needed to, but that didn't make it any easier.

Being forced to work in the hot sun like that was almost like torture.

#1: Storage of Hazardous Materials

Wood Intermediate School uses the detention room to store radioactive waste. That's a bold statement, I know, but the facts don't lie.

There are metal cans stacked in the back all willy-nilly, and the room REEKS of fumes, but the principal doesn't care. Why would he? Out of sight, out of mind, I'm sure, but I've seen enough movies to know that the careless storage of radioactive ooze is how the ZOMBIE APOCALYPSE begins!

EPISODE 10:
A QUICK UPDATE

THIS WILL BE SHORT BECAUSE I'M SUPPOSED TO BE GETTING READY FOR SCHOOL...

▶ ❙❙

Ø4 VIEWS   4 FANS

But some things are just too important to ignore.

First up – for those of you hanging in suspense, I'd like to report that Dutch McKenzie has NOT tried seeking revenge on me for the whole taco thing.

To be honest, I was scared. Like, really scared. I spent all night peeking out the motel window all paranoid, but then I realized if he was gonna do something, he would've done it by now.

Right?

At least, that's what I'm banking on. So I guess I'm in the clear. I mean, it's not like I'm gonna ask him about it because I don't want to accidentally remind him just in case he forgot.

56

And the second, more important thing, is that I have TWO new Fans, which brings my total to THREE!

Okay, it's actually FOUR, but one of those is Fergus and he doesn't count. The first one was Chuck. And my two new Fans today were my mom, and somebody with the username CoolDad81.

Congratulations, CoolDad81, because you can officially say you followed me BEFORE I became a massive Internet sensation! If I had any merchandise, I'd sign it and sell it to you at a discount, but I can't because I don't.

EPISODE 11:
THE GREAT YETI HUNT

Well, not really, because I don't think the Yeti exists, but what do I know? I'm an expert in many things, but make-believe monsters ISN'T one of those things. For some reason, I just don't care about make-believe monsters that people take blurry photos of. Annie, however, LOVES it.

So Chuck and I thought it'd be pretty funny if we tricked her into thinking the Yeti lives in the woods behind the motel. It wouldn't be hard because Chuck's got an old bear costume from Halloween. It even came with boots that makes paw prints on the ground.

We just needed to give Annie a reason to believe the Yeti was nearby. We had to be subtle. If we pushed TOO hard, then it'd be obvious we were making it all up.

That's all it took to make Annie obsess about it during school, and by the end of the day, it was actually HER idea to go on a Yeti hunt.

I was surprised at how easy it was to get her to do what I wanted. Actually, now that I think about it, I'm not that surprised. Anybody who believes in monsters is probably pretty gullible. It was either that, or I'm just THAT good at lying.

I wouldn't put it past me to be awesome at something like that.

Chuck and I came up with a simple plan. He'd run around the woods in the bear costume, while I led Annie on an expedition to find him. Then, after the sun went down, Chuck would turn the tables and start chasing after US.

The hunt started the second we got home. The three of us packed a bunch of stuff into a bag and went out to the woods behind the motel. But just as we got there, Chuck PRETENDED to sprain his ankle so he could leave and get into his bear costume.

I acted like I was bummed, but only because Annie needed to believe it was for real. She totally fell for it, too, because I'm kind of a naturally talented actor. Not to toot my own horn or anything, but when I was in 2nd grade, I had the LEAD role in a Sunday School play about Noah's Ark.

And no, I WASN'T Noah.

I was God.

After Chuck left, my only goal was to keep Annie on the brink of catching him. All I had to do was dangle the Yeti in front of her face to keep her moving forward just like people used to do with carrots while riding on horses. That thought actually gave me a great idea, too, but Annie wasn't on board.

NO,
YOU CAN'T
RIDE ON MY
BACK!

As long there weren't any unexpected hiccups, the rest of the prank would've been awesome. Except, of course, there had to be a hiccup. There's ALWAYS a hiccup.

That's when I heard some cracking branches behind the bushes. I couldn't see what was out there, but I could tell it was coming closer. It couldn't have been Chuck because he was supposed to wait until dark before turning against us, which meant it must've been SOMETHING ELSE.

Like a mountain lion or something.

Not that there's a ton of mountain lions hanging around cities, but I've seen enough nightly news to know they should at least be on my radar.

Annie looked at me like, "What do we do?" but I was already at the top of a tree. It all happened so fast, I'm not even sure how I got up there.

Annie picked up a rock and threw it at the bush where the noise was coming from. I expected a monstrous roar, but what we got instead was more of an "Ouch!" sound.

It was from the very last person in the world that I wanted to see. Fergus Widdershim.

I think we would've been better off with a mountain lion.

Apparently, Annie thought it was a great idea to invite Fergus WITHOUT asking me if I was cool with it. Obviously, I WASN'T cool with it, which is probably why she didn't ask, but that doesn't matter because she SHOULD'VE asked!

And then he had the NERVE to set up his camera RIGHT IN FRONT OF ME, like I wasn't already in the middle of my OWN video shoot!

I kept telling him we had it under control and that he could leave, but Annie told him to stay because we could use an extra set of eyes. Fergus obviously agreed with her, but why wouldn't he?

I knew what he was secretly up to.

The hunt for the Yeti was a great idea and Fergus was just trying to mooch off me to get some views for HIS channel. That's so lame, but if I would've said anything about it to Annie, she probably would've thrown a fit.

And then to top it all off, Fergus busted out his drone. You know what that is, right? It's a little remote-controlled helicopter with a camera on the bottom so you can record video in the air.

Joke's on him because his drone was totally unnecessary for finding the Yeti since it WASN'T ACTUALLY OUT THERE.

But what actually WAS out there was Chuck, and we needed to start moving before he got bored waiting for us.

If that happened, then we'd be in the woods all night looking for him while he was back in his bedroom playing videogames. No offense to that kid, but he's got the attention span of a gnat.

So, the three of us started searching for a monster that doesn't even exist. Well, DOESN'T EXIST that we KNOW of.

Don't wanna offend anybody who believes he's real.

Apologies to any Yeti enthusiasts out there.

Anyways, it didn't take long to find Chuck's footprints because he BARELY went into the woods like he was supposed to. We only walked for about a minute before Annie spotted him practicing ninja kicks on a tree.

We were so close that we could hear him counting, which was SO frustrating because I'm pretty sure the Yeti doesn't know kung-fu OR how to count.

At that point, our total time spent in the woods was about 15 minutes. We still had FIVE hours until the sun went down, and Chuck was ALREADY messing things up!

I wasn't really sure what to do next because my plan never involved actually catching up to Chuck, so I froze up while Annie started throwing rocks as hard as she could at the ninja Yeti.

The first few rocks got Chuck's attention, but the ones after that got his head. He tried to run, but his giant monster feet tripped him up and he fell flat on his chest. You wouldn't know it by looking at her, but Annie can throw a rock like a pro. Chuck was screaming for her to stop, but she must not have heard him because she started throwing them faster.

68

Chuck was NOT happy.

He took off his mask and threw it on the ground, and then he tried to kick it at us like it was a soccer ball, but missed and landed on his back, which only made him madder.

Annie was laughing so hard that she was crying. I think she knew it was Chuck the whole time because she didn't act surprised, but I'm 100% sure that Fergus was clueless.

EPISODE 11:
GRANNY'S GOT SKILLS

THIS MORNING, I WATCHED AN OLD COUPLE CHECK OUT OF THE MOTEL...

▶ ❚❚   [CC] ✳ [▯▫] [ ]

Ø4 VIEWS   4 FANS

They were moving slowly, probably so they wouldn't break their hips or something. Those things shatter like glass after a certain age.

Chuck even had to help take their bags to their car, which he was totally cool with because he's kind of a gentleman like that.

I would've helped, too, but I had a camera in my hands.

They were the kind of old couple you see on the TV news because they've been married since before TVs were invented.

Or at least before COLOR TVs were invented.

They were also the kind of old couple who hated being on camera.

And as they were yelling at me, I had this thought – how hilarious would it be if the woman busted out a skateboard and did cool tricks all over the parking lot?

So that's what gave me the idea for THIS episode – THE SKATEBOARDING GRANDMA! All I needed was a skateboard and a dress. Lucky for me, Chuck had the skateboard, and my mom had a dress I could borrow.

The best place to pull a stunt like that is at the mall on a Saturday afternoon. There'd be plenty of open space and tons of unsuspecting shoppers.

My dad took me and Chuck to the mall right after it opened. I had to wear the dress under my regular clothes so my dad wouldn't see it because I'm pretty sure he'd have a problem with me skating around in one of my mom's fancy party dresses. It's not like she doesn't have TONS of them, though.

Chuck and I went straight to the food court to find a table to set up my camera, but most of them were taken. And the empty tables had jackets on them, which meant they were taken, too.

It was pretty obvious who the jackets belonged to.

It took a few minutes for me to get ready because I wanted everything to be perfect. I took off my top layer of clothes and put them on a table that had a bunch of jackets on it, but only because I knew we'd be done before they got back.

Chuck got out my wig, which was the hairpiece from the bear mask he used for the Yeti prank. It was a little wonky from all the rocks Annie had thrown at it, but that only made it look MORE real, like I was a witch or something.

I drew some wrinkles on my face with a black marker and then I added the finishing touch on my feet for maximum believability, the "piece de resistance," as my dad would say, but I don't know why it's called that since it's not resisting anything.

Anyways, it's THAT kind of attention to detail that wins awards.

Camera? Check. Costume? Check. Audience? Check.

Lights. Camera. Action.

First things first – I needed to convince everyone that I was an old woman BEFORE the skateboarding part, so I hobbled around like I had a bad back.

OH, HEAVENS
TO BETSY,
HEAVENS
TO BETSY...

HEAAAAAVENS
TO BETSY, HEAVENS
TO BETSY!

But my acting skills were so good that every time I started to lean over, some random old person would break away from his mall-walker squad to help me because he thought I was gonna fall over for real.

It was a different guy every time. He'd hold my hand and everything. And they were all SO happy for their random act of kindness that I couldn't bring myself to break out the skateboard because I didn't want them to die from embarrassment. I know what that feels like, and I just couldn't do it.

That happened over and over. Again and again. For THIRTY minutes.

CAN YOU SKATE SOON?
SO FAR, THE ONLY FOOTAGE
WE HAVE IS A BUNCH OF OLD
GUYS HELPING YOU WALK.

And then I had my chance. The first time someone DIDN'T help me find a seat, I whipped the skateboard out from under my dress and hopped on top.

Just so you know, that was the first time in my life I'd ever been on a skateboard. I figured it couldn't be THAT hard because it's got four wheels, so it's not like you have to keep your balance. All you have to do is STAND on it while it rolls.

Chuck's skateboard must've been defective because as soon as I put both feet on the it, the thing flew out from under me like a missile. It shot across the floor and went airborne! That sucker flew over people's heads until it slammed into a vending machine.

The glass didn't break, THANKFULLY, but the crash had everybody looking. It was attention, but not the kind I wanted. I realized I needed to book it before mall security showed up, but I was too late.

A mall security guard rolled in on a Segway, but he was no match for my chameleon-like skills. I blended in perfectly with a group of mall-walkers, and the guard flew right past me without a clue.

Chuck and I made a clean getaway, but we still had TWO HOURS until my dad was supposed to come back and get us because, for some reason, I thought the whole skateboarding thing would take longer than thirty minutes.

My normal clothes were still back in the food court, but there was no way I was going back there because you NEVER return to the scene of a crime.

...not that what I did was a crime or anything.

So anyways, there I was, stuck in my mom's fancy dress with nothing else to do but walk around the mall. And it actually wasn't THAT awful. I mean, at first it was awkward, but then it got fun once I realized Chuck was more uncomfortable with it than I was.

After about an hour, Chuck and I found a store called Hacktronics. It sold all kinds of cool things like laptops and videogames. But most importantly, it had drones.

I've been thinking a lot about this, and I've decided that I definitely NEED a drone. My dad says there's a difference between "WANTING something" and "NEEDING something," but that's just his way of not WANTING to spend any money.

You see, my problem is that my videos are GREAT, but they're not AMAZING yet. And I KNOW drone footage would be the solution to that problem.

HACKTRONICS

YOU ONLY WANT ONE BECAUSE FERGUS HAS ONE.

YOU SAY THAT LIKE IT'S A BAD THING.

I'm honest enough to admit that Fergus' videos look a TINY BIT better than mine, but it's BECAUSE he has a drone. And, right now, it's the ONLY explanation I have for why he's doing better than me. I know I've been kind of obsessing over it, but seriously! It's not like he's funnier than me or anything!

DAVY JUST GIVES ME A HARD TIME BECAUSE THAT'S WHAT REAL BUDDIES DO! AND HE'S THE **BEST** AT IT! HE'S **SO** FUNNY!

Anyways, there must've been twenty different drones in Hacktronics. The smallest ones were ten bucks, but they didn't record video. The ones behind glass cases were over a thousand dollars, which was a little out of my budget.

And then I saw it.

RAPTOR
$99.99

It's the same drone Fergus has.

The Raptor was $99.99, but that's about $50 more than I have saved up. I asked an employee named Karen if drones ever went on sale, but she said they almost never do, so I'd have to pay full price... unless I got a store credit card.

OUR HACKTRONICS CREDIT CARD OFFERS A 10% SENIOR DISCOUNT, MA'AM.

OH, NO, HE'S WEARING A COST—

THAT SOUNDS LIKE A SWELL IDEA, YOUNG LADY!

I was almost positive that wasn't gonna work, but I had to try or else I'd have to live the rest of my life wondering, "What if...?"

And I ALMOST got away with it. I was halfway through the application when Karen figured out I WASN'T an eighty-year-old woman. But that was only because my wig fell off when I bent over to adjust my heels. Those things were KILLING my little toesies.

That was awkward.

UH...
HEHE...

Chuck and I were asked to leave, but we needed to get going anyways. It had been about two hours since my dad dropped us off so he was waiting for us outside with my mom and my sister.

I completely forgot that I was still wearing my mom's dress until she started flipping out about it.

I told her I was only wearing it because my regular clothes were stolen, but that just made my dad flip out, too. Then my sister joined in, just because, and I pretty much got yelled at by my whole family on the drive back to the motel.

I got grounded with an early bedtime, but that's not as easy as it sounds when your whole family shares the same room. So my mom made me a bed in the bathtub and pulled the shower curtain shut, which made it super gross for me when someone had to use the toilet.

I was so CLOSE to getting that Raptor. I know if I try REALLY hard, I can get it. All I need is $50! I'll just have to figure out a way to make some extra cash.

I might even be able to make a little money on these videos by putting commercials in them. People do it all the time. I'm not sure how much I'll get paid, but as long as the ads aren't long or boring, they shouldn't be a big deal.

Ø4 VIEWS   4 FANS

EPISODE 11:
HOW TO GET RICH QUICK

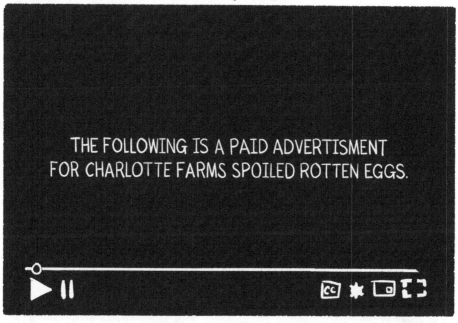

THE FOLLOWING IS A PAID ADVERTISMENT
FOR CHARLOTTE FARMS SPOILED ROTTEN EGGS.

HERE AT CHARLOTTE FARMS, WE PRIDE OURSELVES
FOR HAVING ONLY THE HIGHEST QUALITY EGGS
IN THE WORLD, AND WE GUARANTEE IT.

YOU MIGHT ASK YOURSELF, HOW CAN THEY GUARANTEE THAT? ARE THEY CRAZY? HA HA HA! WELL, WE **ARE** CRAZY - CRAZY ABOUT EGGS!

YOU SEE, CHARLOTTE FARMS SPOILED ROTTEN EGGS START WITH OUR SPOILED ROTTEN CHICKENS. YOU WON'T FIND ANY CHICKEN COOPS HERE.

EACH HEN HAS HER OWN FULLY FURNISHED,
LUXURIOUS APARTMENT WHERE THEY GET TO KICK
BACK AND RELAX AFTER A LONG DAY OF PAMPERING.

A STAFF OF MASSAGE THERAPISTS HELP OUR
CHICKENS ALLEVIATE STRESS, WHICH ENSURES A VERY
TENDER EGG YOLK AND A PRETTY HAPPY HEN.

A WORLD CLASS, PROFESSIONAL CHEF PREPARES EVERY MEAL, SPECIFICALLY CATERED TO EACH HEN'S DIETARY NEEDS.

ONLY $199.99 PER DOZEN! ORDER NOW!

TRY OUR SPOILED ROTTEN EGGS TODAY AND TASTE THE CHARLOTTE FARMS DIFFERENCE.

WHAT IN THE HECK WAS THAT??

THAT'S the commercial they put on my videos?? That thing was FIVE-MINUTES long! Who wants to watch chickens getting pampered for FIVE WHOLE MINUTES??

Okay, I'm definitely pulling the plug on that whole thing. I promise my channel will be commercial-free from now on.

They're such a lame way for videos to make money anyway. I mean, just take me to the content, right?

The good stuff. That's what we want to see. Not a bunch of chickens getting backrubs and eating fancier food than us.

I mean, if I wanted to watch commercials, I'd watch regular TV like some kind of caveman.

But just to be perfectly clear, I'm still open to the idea of CORPORATE SPONSORSHIPS. If any company wants to throw money at me for putting their stuff in my videos, please please please send me an email.

Anyways, this morning I made the mistake of asking my dad for fifty bucks right after he woke up, which, now that I think about it, was the worst time to ask.

I should've known better. The best time to ask is when he's on the couch after dinner, but it's not like I can do that since we don't have a couch right now.

The good news is that he didn't say no. But the bad news is that he also didn't say yes. He gave me an answer that isn't actually an answer at all. I think you know what I'm talking about. He said...

That's just a nicer way of saying, "Go away." And asking my mom after my dad says that only gets me into trouble, so I left her out of it.

Without my parents help, I was on my own, and making money is hard for sixth graders. Why? Because we're SIXTH GRADERS. If I wanted money, I'd have to get creative. Good thing CREATIVE just happens to be my middle name.

The first thing I tried was giving dollar haircuts in the back of the boy's locker room. If I had more experience, I would've charged more, but the only haircut I knew how to give was the kind that involved a bowl. I made six bucks before kids figured out what was happening.

The second thing I tried was selling candy out of my luggage. I know the school sells candy from vending machines, but those are only in the cafeteria, and kids can't use them unless it's during lunch or study hall. But my candy was available any time of the day, all day long.

I have to admit my idea was pretty great because it didn't cost me a single penny. I just used my dad's secret stash of full-sized candy bars that he kept in our motel closet in case of emergencies.

To get business moving, I offered MY candy for cheaper than the vending machines. I sold everything I had for only a quarter apiece, which is a STEAL.

And then sales REALLY took off when I said that price was only good until the end of the school day. At one point, a line of kids formed behind me before I even knew it.

My pockets were FULL of quarters, but all the attention started to worry me because it was just too much. I'd walk into a room, and the whole class would quiet down and watch me take my seat because they all knew what I was up to.

I wasn't sure if selling candy bars out of my carry-on was illegal or not, but I suddenly got this weird feeling in my stomach like I was doing something wrong. It got so bad that I even asked my social studies teacher, Mrs. Hernandez, a question that was eating away at me.

By lunch, I swear that Chad Schulte, a hall monitor, had started following me around. Every time I looked over my shoulder, he was there with his back turned, wearing those extra wide spy sunglasses with the little mirrors on the edges so he can watch people without being suspicious.

Even though I was selling TONS of candy, I HATED feeling paranoid, so I ran into a bathroom and dumped my stash into the garbage before Chad could follow me.

It was just in time, too, because he kicked the door open and acted like it was a totally normal thing for him to do.

When I counted my quarters, I realized I didn't make as much as I thought. My pockets were so full that my pants were sagging, but when I added it all up, I found out that I only made about $10.

My last attempt at a "Get Rich Quick" scheme before school let out didn't last very long either. Kids just don't wanna hear the truth.

By the end of the day, I had made $17.25. That's not bad, but it's still not enough for the Raptor.

EPISODE 14:
THE SEARCH FOR MORE MONEY

CHUCK FOUND THIS METAL DETECTOR IN HIS ATTIC, SO...

OBVIOUSLY, we used it to try and find loose change in the parking lot. I was hoping to find some kind of buried treasure, but nope. We were out there for three hours, and all we detected was seventy-five cents and a rusty belt buckle.

MY DAD'S GONNA BE MAD WHEN HE SEES WHAT WE DID.

YOU MEAN WHEN HE SEES WHAT **YOU** DID. **YOU'RE** THE ONE WITH THE SHOVEL.

BEEP BEEP BEEP!!!

EPISODE 15, PART 1:
WHEN LIFE GIVES YOU POWDERED LEMONADE MIX, MAKE LEMONADE

I FIGURED OUT WHY MAKING MONEY AT SCHOOL IS SO HARD. IT'S BECAUSE KIDS DON'T HAVE ANY! REAL MONEY IS WITH ADULTS...

Ø4 VIEWS   4 FANS

And what does every adult need first thing in the morning?

Coffee and Donuts.

Before school, I set up a small table with an assortment of donuts and two pots of coffee, one regular and one decaf, right outside the El Rancho Motel's front office.

If guests wanted to check out, they had to go through me because I had the entrance totally blocked. And the only way I was gonna let them through was if they paid me for a coffee and a donut.

It was a genius move on my part.

But there were a couple of adults who disagreed with my vision, so that idea got shut down pretty quick.

95

I spent the rest of my day brainstorming different business ideas and editing my videos at school. I always zone out during class anyways, so I figured I could use that time to get a lot of work done instead.

It's called "taking initiative," and YOU'D THINK Mr. Mitchell would appreciate a student demonstrating that kind of leadership in front of his peers. But he didn't. He was just annoyed.

And finally, after a bunch of pretty good ideas, one really great idea came to me – a traveling lemonade stand. Allow me to explain...

Lemonade stands are popular because they're easy to start. Kids set up on a street corner and wave to cars that pass by. Sometimes someone stops, but most of the time they don't because they're busy. They're tired. They just wanna get home after a long day of work and be lazy.

THAT'S the problem. In today's world, adults want things DELIVERED to them because of how LAZY they are. They don't wanna GO to a lemonade stand... they want the lemonade stand to come to THEM.

Now, Chuck and I could do things the old-fashioned way by dragging lemonade behind us in a wagon like a couple of farmers, but that's not exactly our style.

We wanted to be modern – no – we wanted to be FUTURISTIC. So Chuck found his Mega Soaker, a huge water gun with a tank you wear on your back. Obviously, we'd fill the tank with lemonade and then shoot it into a cup when a customer wants one. We even thought it'd be cool if we filled two smaller water guns with lemonade so we could shoot out samples.

THAT'S JUST PHASE 1 OF MY PLAN. IN PHASE 2, WE'LL GET SOME BIKES AND DELIVER LEMONADE WATER BALLOONS.

I KNOW.

YOU ARE **SO** SMART.

Besides the water guns, the only supplies we needed for the traveling lemonade stand were the actual lemonade and some cups. Cups were easy. Chuck grabbed a bunch next to the coffee pot in the motel office since I wasn't allowed in there anymore. So then our only problem was the lemonade. We didn't have any. And that's kind of important when you're selling LEMONADE.

BUT... my mom DID have some big boxes of juice in our motel room, made by a company called "Chardonnay." It sounded French. French meant fancy. And fancy meant we could charge more money per cup. But for some reason my mom was completely against that idea.

Anyways, my dad picked up some Kool-Aid Lemonade packets for us on his way home from work. He bought four for a buck, which is crazy cheap because each packet makes a whole pitcher of lemonade.

If we could sell THAT much lemonade, I'd be able to buy that drone before bedtime. I mixed up a batch and poured it into the tank on Chuck's back and we were ready to go.

We started with Annie's house since it was right next door to the motel. It actually turned out to be a good first stop because it turns out that I forgot to add the most important ingredient to the Kool-Aid Lemonade.

Annie's mom was cool. She gave me all the sugar I needed and never asked for her money back.

Annie tagged along with us after that. I thought it was because she wanted to make some extra cash, so I made it perfectly clear that ALL the lemonade money was going toward my drone. She was fine with that, but only because she "needed a break from working on her science project.

We visited every house for two blocks, but only sold 3 cups of lemonade. I mean, come on, it was just a DOLLAR. I can find THAT in my couch cushions, AND I DON'T EVEN HAVE A COUCH.

The most annoying part was when people asked WHY we were selling the lemonade, like we needed a reason or something. I mean, yeah, the REASON was because I wanted a drone, but that's not any of THEIR business. Who are they? The lemonade police?

To try and make things easier for us, I started saying the money was going to help a kid follow his dream, which WASN'T a lie, but THAT only raised MORE questions.

We went a few more blocks before Annie suggested a more aggressive sales approach. It was gonna be dark soon, which meant we'd have to stop because people hate it when strangers knock on their door after 9 at night, don't ask me why.

Annie took the lead for the next house, which had a metal ramp that led to the porch. There was another one on the side of the house, too.

And that's when I saw a large stone sitting next to the front door with the name "WIDDERSHIM" etched into it. Those ramps were for a wheelchair.

EPISODE 15, PART 1: BEHIND ENEMY LINES

SO THERE WE WERE... AT THE HOUSE OF MY OWN ARCHENEMY.

Ø4 VIEWS   4 FANS

I figured we had about fifteen seconds before someone answered the door, and fifteen seconds is a TON of time. In fifteen seconds, you could blow up a balloon, tell a joke, play a quick game of catch, tie your shoes, give somebody a hug, do a little dance...

ALL of those wonderful things!

Listen, the point is - fifteen seconds was more than enough time for us to bail without getting caught. Fergus' family could live the rest of their lives just thinking they got ding-dong-ditched!

But Annie didn't care that we were at Fergus' house.

She just wanted to show us how being more AGGRESSIVE would sell lemonade, so she told us to watch carefully, and then she showed us exactly what she was talking about.

Thankfully, nobody was home. At least, it seemed like that because nobody came to the door. We were already in a bad mood, so it didn't surprise me when we started arguing with each other about why we'd barely sold any lemonade. Annie won but only because she could yell the loudest.

We spent about five minutes on the porch, arguing about whether we should go to one more house or just head back to the motel. I REALLY wish we had spent that time walking AWAY from Fergus' house because, just then... the front door opened.

It was a woman with a phone in her hand, and she was staring right at ME.

And just for the record, I want you to know that I've never met that woman before. I wouldn't be able to point her out in a crowd if you asked me to, so it kind of blew my mind when the first thing she said to me was...

It was Fergus' mom, Mrs. Widdershim. She had been hiding inside the whole time because she was so scared that Annie was trying to break into her house.

She even took notes on our clothes so the police would know who to look for when she dialed 911. LUCKILY she recognized MY face before any of that happened.

Did you hear that? Fergus told his mom ALL ABOUT ME.

Probably because she's just as evil as he is. Their whole FAMILY probably is! That house is probably FULL of people who want to crush my dreams and see me fail.

Mrs. Widdershim shouted for Fergus and then invited us inside. I tried to say no, but Chuck and Annie had already walked through the door, so I HAD to follow them to make sure that wasn't the last time I'd ever see them. Everything about that situation stunk like a trap, and we needed to stick together.

We waited for Fergus in the living room while his mom brought us glasses of chocolate milk. She even put whipped cream on top. Probably poisoned. Maybe not. I don't know. I didn't watch her make the drinks, but I didn't wanna risk it, so I let Chuck and Annie take the first sip.

That's when Fergus came around the corner with a huge smile on his face, like he was happy to see us. But was he though? It's not like he was expecting us. Or WAS he?

Is Fergus that much of a diabolical genius that he could influence the future with microscopic actions in the past? Or what if he was a mind reader?? I decided to test him. If he was reading my mind, then making as much noise as possible in my head SHOULD'VE hurt his ears.

It didn't work.

Anyways, Fergus kept talking about how he was all excited that we came over because nobody ever does and blah blah blah. Yeah, right. I'm sure the most popular YouTubeer at Wood Intermediate has trouble finding friends.

PLEASE.

It was all an act. It HAD to be. I'd caught him off-guard by showing up unannounced and he panicked because I'd slipped through his defenses and infiltrated his home base.

And then I thought maybe being inside Fergus' house was a good thing. If I could sneak away from everybody, I could find his computer and learn his secrets like I was some kind of spy. I just needed a good excuse to get out of the living room.

And then I could look around on my own. There wasn't a second floor, but it was possible that his studio could be in the basement. Go figure. Most villains have underground lairs.

But then Fergus must've read my mind – AGAIN – because he was one step ahead of me.

So the three of us followed Fergus down the hall and into a room where I expected to see a full studio with dozens of cameras and a bunch of kids slaving away on his videos.

I was actually surprised to see NONE of that.

It was just an empty room with a giant exercise ball, some dumbbells, and a yoga mat. The only video equipment he had was a laptop connected to a camera, sitting on a small desk in the corner. On the floor was his Raptor drone.

Fergus opened a picture on his laptop and showed us how he put cool special effects in his videos. It actually didn't look too hard, and the program he used was free, but why would he show me that? Wouldn't he want to keep that kind of stuff secret from me? I know I'd keep it secret from HIM.

He showed us some other tricks, too, like making things slow-motion and adding background music. He made it look easy, but I knew it wasn't.

That kind of stuff takes a ton of time to figure out, especially when you're doing it all by yourself. Fergus didn't have a camera crew or a NASA-style super-computer. All he had was a laptop and a camera.

Just like me.

And that's when I realized that Fergus was never trying to send me a message. He was never trying to tell me ANYTHING because he was too busy busting his own chops to make great videos. I wanted to learn all his secrets, but all I ended up learning was...

EPISODE 16:
I SMASHED A HORNET'S NEST

IT'S BEEN A ROUGH COUPLE OF DAYS SINCE FERGUS' HOUSE. BUT NOT BECAUSE OF WHAT HAPPENED THERE. IT WAS BECAUSE OF WHAT HAPPENED AFTER.

The day after Fergus showed us his laptop there was a knock at our door. It was Chuck's parents, and they were NOT happy about all the holes in their parking lot from when Chuck and I were looking for loose change.

I told my parents that it was so I could buy the drone. I knew it wouldn't let me off the hook, but I thought I could at least score some points for being financially mature.

It didn't end up helping at all.

Obviously.

So I apologized. Chuck's parents were really nice about it, which was really cool of them. All they wanted was the apology. And the whole thing would've stopped right there, but my dad had to go and open his big mouth and say...

Chuck's parents thought that was a GREAT idea, and that's how I spent the longest weekend of my life – as a victim of child labor.

It took about half a day to fill in all the holes we dug because there were so many of them. The seventy-five cents we found was definitely NOT worth it.

And it was hot outside, too, but not just A LITTLE hot. It was A LOT of hot – the kind of hot where they tell the newborn babies and the elderly to stay indoors. It was so hot that Chuck started seeing things that weren't there.

And then, RIGHT after we fixed the parking lot, we had to take care of a hornet's nest. I was expecting something small, maybe as big as a golf ball or something, but nope. The nest was the size of my HEAD.

AND DAVY'S HEAD IS **HUGE**. SERIOUSLY, IT'S LIKE A SMALL PLANET!

I almost had a panic attack because I'm deathly afraid of ANY insect that can grow a weapon out of its body. I'm not allergic or anything – it's just that I don't like getting stung.

I mean, does anybody?

Mr. Metropolis didn't even give us any kind of armor for our battle with the hornets, so we had to find some ourselves.

We searched for thirty minutes, but all we came up with was a hockey stick, a pool skimmer to put over our head, and some dishwashing gloves. It probably wasn't the best protection, but it was better than nothing.

Chuck and I played rock, paper, scissors to see who would attack the nest. Of course, I was the one who lost, but only because that game doesn't make any sense when you think about it.

Chuck and Annie watched from the other side of a motel room window just in case something bad happened, which, big surprise, it did.

Did you know hornets hate it when their nest gets whacked by a hockey stick? That's right, you did. Everybody knows that because it's knowledge you're born with. It's called "instinct."

The rest of the weekend was spent mowing the El Rancho motel's lawn. It's not that big so it should've been an easy job, but I don't think cutting ANY grass is easy when you're using an ANTIQUE lawnmower.

That's all Mr. Metropolis had because he always hires professionals to do the work for him. The mower didn't even have an engine! You were supposed to push it forward to spin the blades! It was probably the same thing George Washington used to mow HIS lawn!

And since there was only one lawnmower, Chuck and I had to take turns using it. Well, it was more like we were taking turns NOT using it.

And by the end of Sunday night, I was completely worn out. I had blisters on my palms, hornet stings on my arms, and grass up my nose. My whole body felt like Jell-O that someone dropped on the floor.

Physical labor HURTS.

But... my parents were proud. They had never seen me work so hard in my life, and I guess it hit a soft spot with both of them.

116

After I showered and got dressed, I walked out to see a surprise waiting for me on the bed, perfectly placed so I wouldn't miss it.

EPISODE 17:
MY FIRST DRONE FLIGHT... YOU WON'T BELIEVE WHAT HAPPENS NEXT,

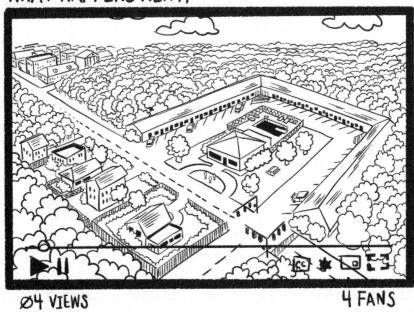

Ø4 VIEWS   4 FANS

EPISODE 18:
CAN ANYBODY HEAR ME?

It's been a week since I broke the drone, and my mom and dad still don't know. They haven't asked about it yet, which is fine by me because I'm too young to die. But Krissy knows. She saw the whole thing when it happened, but she didn't tell on me because she's an evil, manipulative creature who's gonna use it to get whatever she wants, which is exactly the kind of thing I would've done. She's more like me than I'd like to admit.

My secret is safe with her, but only if I rub her feet until she falls asleep at night. And for the rest of the school year. And maybe all next summer. But to be fair, she definitely needs it after a long day of doing NOTHING.

Right after "THE INCIDENT" (that's what we're calling it now – tell your friends), I got all the pieces of the drone together to try and fix it but couldn't. It wasn't just a cracked shell or something small like that – the whole thing was shattered because I dive-bombed it into the parking lot.

But I didn't want to throw it away, so I hid it under my parent's bed. It's the one place I know they'll never look. They're such germaphobes that I'm almost 100% sure they'll never check under there. They're too afraid of what they'll find in the dark places of a motel room.

And before you say anything, I already know that vlogging about all this stuff probably isn't the smartest thing to do because my parents might see the videos, right?

Well, I'm not too worried about that either since neither of them watch my vlog. I'm actually beginning to think NOBODY does. It's probably the best thing I've ever worked on, and NOBODY EVEN CARES.

EPISODE 19:
THE SADDEST CLOWN IN THE WORLD

I had to go to a picnic dinner for my dad's office tonight. Not only me, but my mom and sister, too. And the funny thing is that NOBODY else in my family wanted to go either. Not even my DAD.

I'm not really sure what my dad's job is. I wanna say it has something to do with computers and drawing, but I'm not sure if that was his old job, and now he's got a different job? Maybe that's why we moved? I feel like that's something I should know, but... I don't.

When we got to the picnic, it looked like we were the last ones there because the only parking space we could find was in the grass at the edge of the park. I'm actually not sure if it was a real parking spot, or if my dad had just given up.

My mom made me carry a cheesy potato casserole that she bought from the store and then dumped in a plastic Tupperware so it looked like she was the one who made it.

My parents told me and my sister to "go play" so they could hang out with other adults. They never said it, but I think they wanted to make some new friends, too, which has to be weird for grownups. I can't really see my parents asking other people if they want to "go play."

Krissy had it easy, but most four-year-olds do. All she had to do was find out where the rest of the preschoolers were, and then jump in like she belonged there.

CANNONBALL!!

There were other middle schoolers I could have joined, but I didn't because I needed to film the very last video ever for my vlog. That's right. I'm not normally a quitter, but what's the point of art if nobody ever looks at it?

So I grabbed a hot dog and found an empty bench. Then I started painting my face like a sad clown using some makeup that I secretly borrowed from my mom.

It was Annie's idea. She said it would it'd be a "powerful insight into my carnival of distress." At first, I didn't believe her, but then I realized that clowns were part of carnivals, so yeah, it kind of made perfect sense. She really DOES know what she's talking about when it comes to stuff like that. She's a REAL artist.

So I dug into my hot dog and filmed myself eating like some kind a whacko with a camera. Kids stopped and stared, but whatever. I didn't care. As soon as I was done, I'd wash off the makeup and say goodbye to my vlog.

And right when I swallowed my last bite, the craziest random thing ever to happen in the universe happened.

Emma Walsh showed up and sat next to me on the bench.

Remember Emma? She's the cool, cute girl that had the locker next to my first one? The one I had for literally one minute before Dutch took it from me. I didn't know Emma was gonna be at that picnic. And if I did, I WOULDN'T HAVE PAINTED MY FACE LIKE A SAD CLOWN!

Emma didn't say anything for a REALLY long time. She just sat there eating her food and watching everybody else at the picnic. She looked up and smiled at me a couple times, but I didn't know what that meant!

And I didn't say anything either because I didn't want to say something stupid that would make her walk away. I was already halfway to stupidville because of my makeup. I mean, how do I explain that without sounding like a total nutcase?

Lucky for me, I didn't have to because, right at that second, she said...

Okay, how the heck would she know about my broken drone? Chuck, Annie, and my sister were the only ones who knew about it, and none of them would've said anything to anyone unless...

She was messing with me. She HAD to be. I only had FOUR fans, and EMMA definitely WASN'T one of them. It's just my mom, Chuck, Fergus, and some guy named...

I was so FLABBERGASTED that I had to look up a new word to describe how I felt.

I couldn't believe it. Emma was telling the truth. She really WAS a Fan. So I got at least ONE KID at school to watch my videos. I could get more, right?

Suddenly, I didn't feel like quitting the vlog anymore. If getting one Fan at a time is what it takes to get famous, then that's what I'll do. I mean, I was already one Fan closer with Emma, and she's one of the most popular kids in school.

HOW COOL IS THAT?

Too bad I didn't have any time to soak it in because she kinda dropped a bomb on me right after that. All I can say is that it's a good thing I was filming because I don't really remember much of anything after this next part.

Yeah. That happened.

When I woke up, there was a crowd around me, and my parents were by my side. As if blacking out while wearing sad clown makeup wasn't bad enough, my mom had taken my shirt off and was pouring water on my naked chest because she thought I overheated.

Oh, right, and Emma was still there, too, watching my mom give me a bath in front of everyone at the picnic. It sounds like something from a nightmare, but I have video evidence that it wasn't just in my head.

Oh, well. That's life, right? It could've been worse, I suppose, because it's not like I had LESS THAN A DAY to make a science fair project from scratch.

Oh, wait, that's EXACTLY what I have to do.

EPISODE 20:
PANIC IN THE BATHROOM

SO... I'VE BEEN UP ALL NIGHT WORKING ON MY SCIENCE FAIR PROJECT.

5:02 AM

After my family left the picnic last night, I asked if we could stop at the craft store because I needed poster board and markers for my science project. My dad said it would have to wait until the morning because it was so late at night.

I'M SURE THERE'S PLENTY OF TIME. WHEN IS IT DUE?

...TOMORROW.

TOMORROW??

I told them that Mr. Mitchell only gave us one day to prepare, but they saw right through me. So I fessed up and said I had a whole month to do it but forgot because I was too busy making videos.

They were NOT happy about that.

Obviously.

My dad stopped at the store and gave me twenty bucks, and my mom begged me to hurry because it was past Krissy's bedtime and my sister was already starting to lose it.

JOHHHHN JACOB JINGLEHEIMER SCHMIIIIDT!!! THAAAAT'S MY NAME, TOOOOOO!!!

So I went into the craft store and found what I needed. The whole place was empty up until I went up front to pay. Then somehow 50 people suddenly appeared and were standing in line for the ONE register that was open. That's alright though. I needed that time to think.

I had no idea what I was gonna do for my project. With less than a day, I don't think I have many options anyways. The good thing is that I don't need an A+ to pass, so my project doesn't need to be AWESOME. It just needs to be good enough. And I'm pretty good at being good enough.

I ended up pulling an all-nighter in the bathroom. It was the only room we had where I could keep the light on and shut the door so I wouldn't wake Krissy or my parents.

EPISODE 21:
MY 6TH GRADE SCIENCE FAIR

I couldn't even think straight during school. Faces became blurry. Words didn't make sense. I was freezing cold, but sweating at the same time, and I was out of breath just sitting in my chair. And then something occurred to me in the hallway...

It got so bad that I went to Ms. Rodriguez, the school nurse, before third period because, at that point, everything was spinning in slow motion.

Thankfully, she said I wasn't gonna die. I was just exhausted. She let me lay down for a minute, but when I opened my eyes, school was almost out. I slept through FOUR classes AND lunch. And then she gave me a couple cookies and a juice box before sending me to 7th period. I'll just say this – Ms. Rodriguez is the COOLEST NURSE EVER and definitely DESERVES a raise.

The science fair started at six-o-clock after school in the gymnasium, which gave me plenty of time to add some finishing touches to my project.

Not that I did, but at least the option was there.

My dad dropped me off at the school a little early so I could sign-in and find a spot in the gym. A bunch of other kids were there early, too, setting up their projects on the lunch tables. Some of them were big and fancy, but a bunch were pretty sad looking, which made me feel better about my own.

And I have to say that once I got everything set up, my project actually kinda looked pretty good.

There was only one project that stuck out above everyone else's. I don't think it'll come as much of a surprise to you to know whose it was.

Fergus. Freaking. Widdershim.

When Annie got there, she set up right next to me. Her project was about making edible sugar crystals. It was obvious that she put a lot more work into hers than I did with mine, but comparing projects was unfair, especially since Annie had a whole month to prepare.

SO DID YOU!

NO. I ONLY HAD ONE NIGHT.

BUT THAT'S YOUR FAULT!

THAT DOESN'T MAKE IT LESS TRUE.

Mr. Mitchell announced the start of the science fair as soon as the clock hit six. That's when teachers started walking down different aisles, taking notes on each kid's project.

And as Annie and I waited for our judgment to come, we heard a voice come from under our table. It was Chuck in his ninja clothes, mask over his face and everything. He was babbling on about needing to hide or something, I don't know, he's really hard to understand when he wears his mask.

Like, seriously hard.

So Annie pulled it off his head and told him to start over. That time, I could understand him... but really wished I still couldn't.

I looked around the gym until I saw Dutch's science fair project all the way on the other side of the room. There wasn't much to it, but the message was clear. I was actually impressed with how straight-forward it was.

Dutch was gonna duct tape me to the wall in front of everyone at the science fair. It was his payback for splattering a taco on his head, and THAT kind of revenge goes in the history books FOREVER.

That's NOT what I wanted to be famous for.

I couldn't see Dutch anywhere in the gymnasium, which was a VERY bad thing because it probably meant that he was already watching me, waiting for the perfect moment to pounce.

I ran like my life depended on it because it kinda did. Not my ACTUAL life, but my SOCIAL life. Dutch pulled out a strip of duct tape and chased after me as I jumped on top of the tables, smashing my way through everybody's science fair projects.

Kids were shouting at me, but I didn't care because I was being chased by a lunatic.

Everybody would understand if they just took a second to see what was happening to me! I leapt from table to table to get away, but Dutch was behind me the whole time. I couldn't lose him if I tried, and trust me, I was TRYING.

I burst through the gym doors into the hallway where the lights were all off because nobody was supposed to be in that part of the school. It was dark and creepy, but I had to find somewhere to hide before Dutch caught up with me.

But all the classroom doors were locked, and there was nowhere for me to go. At that point, I would've locked MYSELF in a locker to get away from that kid.

And then someone shouted at me from all the way down the hall. It was Fergus, and he was lit up like an angel from the light inside the elevator that he was holding open.

For a moment, I wondered if Fergus and Dutch were working together to trap me. Dutch would get to duct tape me to the inside of the elevator, probably leaving me there overnight, and Fergus would get a hilarious video out of it.

I barely had any time to think about it though because that's when Dutch slammed through the gym doors and slid to a stop behind me. He looked like some kind of monster in the dark hallway.

It was hard, but I sucked it up, pushed my hatred for Fergus deep into the pit of my stomach, and did the thing everybody tells you not to do... I went towards the light.

I ran faster than I've ever run in my life and dove into the elevator just as the doors shut, but Fergus didn't push the #2 button for the second floor. Instead, he pressed his finger to his lips to keep me quiet as we listened to Dutch's squeaking sneakers fade away.

It was smart because Dutch was gonna be there when the elevator opened upstairs, but we weren't gonna be inside. All we had to do was wait long enough so he wouldn't see us go back into the gym. It was the perfect escape plan.

Except for the fact that it didn't work.

Fergus waited about thirty seconds, and then he pushed the button to open the elevator doors, but they didn't budge. Instead, a little bell dinged, and the whole thing started going UP.

Clearly, we underestimated how quickly Dutch could get to the second floor.

150

The giant metal box was taking me straight to my doom, and it was ALL FERGUS' FAULT. If that nub had pushed the button ONE SECOND SOONER, my short little life wouldn't have been flashing before my eyes.

I thought about all the videos I'd never make. All the fans I'd never meet. All the highs I'd never five. All the girls I'd never go out with.

The elevator jerked to a stop, and the doors opened. Sure enough, Dutch was right outside with strips of duct tape hanging from his hands.

SHRRRP!

And then the craziest thing happened.

Fergus rolled his wheelchair out of the elevator to keep Dutch from getting to me. Every move Dutch made, Fergus blocked by rolling back and forth.

He didn't have to tell ME twice.

I jumped out of the elevator and ran down the hall as Fergus grabbed Dutch's arm and held him back. Honestly, I don't know why Fergus was helping me. It wasn't like we were friends. I would've NEVER done that for him if the tables were turned.

I was at the stairs when I heard the sound of metal crash against metal, and I knew what it was without even looking.

I turned around and saw Fergus in his wheelchair, pinned against the lockers by Dutch, who was pulling out more strips of duct tape. If he couldn't get to me then I guess he'd settle for someone else.

Fergus has been a headache ever since I met him. He's better at making videos than me, and he rubs it in my face by NEVER bragging about it.

He even gave me advice about how to make MY OWN channel more popular. And I'm pretty sure if I wanted to borrow any of his gear, he'd TOTALLY let me.

He's SO BAD at being the bad guy that he's basically the opposite of that. So let's be real – maybe some kids DESERVE to get taped to the wall. And by that, I mean maybe I'M one of those kids, okay?

All that kid does is try to help me – with videos, with friends, with Dutch. I don't think I've ever seen him NOT smiling. I absolutely hate to admit this, but Fergus is the kind of kid I want to be. Not because he's famous, but because he's a GOOD kid.

And I was just gonna walk away when HE needed help?

I couldn't be that guy.

So I turned around, marched right back to the elevator, and told Dutch to back off of Fergus. If it was me he wanted, then he could have me, but Fergus was off-limits.

I was so brave. So VERY brave. It was the single most BRAVEST thing I'd ever done.

Dutch was cool with it, no surprise there, and when it was all finished, it wasn't as bad as I thought it'd be.

Duct tape is surprisingly strong.

EPISODE 22:
WE DID IT... SORT OF...

14 VIEWS   9 FANS

My face was everywhere. TV. Newspapers. Internet.

I mean, COME ON, right? I heroically sacrificed myself for Fergus, but the only thing everybody can focus on is how I WRECKED the science fair.

I tried explaining the whole "Dutch" situation to Mr. Mitchell and Principal Hawkins, but both of them were more upset at the fact that I didn't find them before things got out of control.

EVEN MY OWN PARENTS didn't care about me getting taped to the wall after they saw what I did in the gymnasium.

I got three days of in-school detention because I broke the science fair projects. Dutch got suspended for two days for duct taping me to the wall.

If you ask me, he got the better end of THAT deal. He gets

to sleep in and watch TV for TWO days. Tell me how that's a fair punishment! Dutch pretty much got a vacation. No wonder he's such a bad guy! It's because he gets rewarded for it while I still have to come to school and hang out with Mr. Garrick for THREE days.

Students with smashed up projects were given an extra week to fix their stuff. Out of the projects that were left standing, Fergus got first place, but I'm glad he did. He deserved it.

Let me also get one thing straight about Fergus so nobody's confused – saving him like I did does NOT make us friends, not even a little bit. I told him that, too, but I'm not so sure he got the message.

And as if all THAT wasn't bad enough, my mom started a YouTube channel for Krissy yesterday and uploaded the video of her having a tea party with her blind dog.

Guess how many views it got OVERNIGHT?

1.2 MILLION!
I'M FAMOUS!!!

Of course that happened.

So anyways, right here is probably the perfect place to end this season. I'm not famous the way I wanted to be, but that's okay. It just means I'll have to try harder next season.

I'm not sure exactly WHEN that'll be since I'm also taking a few days off from vlogging.

I just think it's a good time for a break, y'know?

Maybe I'll find a beach somewhere to relax. Actually, it'll be more like a little grass patch by a creek or something. Doesn't matter. As long as I stay out of trouble, I think I'll be fine...

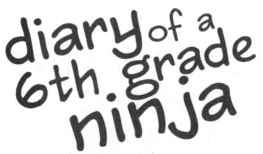

Marcus Emerson is the author of several highly imaginative children's books including DIARY OF A 6th GRADE NINJA series, THE SUPER LIFE OF BEN BRAVER, and RECESS WARRIORS. His goal is to create children's books that are engaging, funny, and inspirational for kids of all ages - even the adults who secretly never grew up.

Marcus Emerson still dreams of becoming an astronaut someday and walking on Mars.

Made in the USA
Monee, IL
08 September 2021